Mr. Jack Is a Maniac!

Dan Gutman

Pictures by

Jim Paillot

HARPER

An Imprint of HarperCollinsPublishers

To Archie and Emi Silverstein

My Weirder School #10: Mr. Jack Is a Maniac!
Text copyright © 2014 by Dan Gutman
Illustrations copyright © 2014 by Jim Paillot
All rights reserved. Printed in the United States of America.
www.harpercollinschildrens.com
ISBN 978-0-06-219841-9 (pbk. bdg.)–ISBN 978-0-06-219842-6 (lib. bdg)
Typography by Kate Engbring
14 15 16 17 OPM 10 9 8 7 6 5 4 3

First Edition

Contents

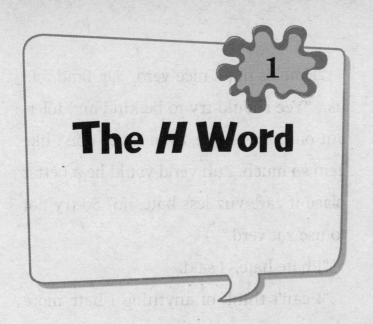

The *H* Word

My name is A.J. and I hate hate.

Let me explain.

It was a really nice day, so Dr. Brad, the school counselor, took our class out to the playground to talk. We sat in a circle near the monkey bars. Dr. Brad was telling us how kids need to be nicer to each other.

1

"'Hate' is not a nice verd," Dr. Brad told us.* "Vee should try to be kind and tolerant of uzzer people, even if vee don't like zem so much. Zuh verld vould be a better place if zare vuz less hate, no? So try not to use zat verd."

"I hate hate," I said.

"I can't think of anything I hate more than hate," said Ryan, who will eat anything, even stuff that isn't food.

"I hate people who hate people," said Michael, who never ties his shoes.

Everybody agreed that they hated hate. Well, everybody except Andrea Young,

---

*Dr. Brad talks funny. If you read this book out loud, make him sound like a crazy German mad scientist.

this annoying girl with curly brown hair.

"If we shouldn't hate things," Andrea said, "then we shouldn't hate hate. Right?"

Huh?

"Yeah, we should *like* hate," said her crybaby friend Emily, who agrees with everything Andrea says.

"But it would be wrong to like hate," said Neil, who we call the nude kid even though he wears clothes.

"I hate hate, but I hate hating hate, too," said Alexia, this girl who rides a skateboard everywhere.

I thought my head was going to explode. I hate when that happens.

"Nobody hates hate more than I hate

hate," said Ryan.

"I hate hate more than *you* hate hate!" said Michael.

"You do not!"

"I do too!"

They went back and forth like that for a while.

"Hate hate hate hate hate hate hate hate," everybody was saying.

"SHTOP ZAYING HATE!" Dr. Brad shouted.

"But *you* just said it!" I told him.

Dr. Brad closed his eyes and rubbed his forehead with his fingers. Did you ever notice that only grown-ups rub their forehead with their fingers? Kids never do that. I guess when you grow up, your forehead gets itchy. Grown-ups are constantly rubbing their forehead with their fingers.

"Zuh point is," said Dr. Brad, "vee should try to use zuh *H* verd less, and *love* each uzzer more."

Everybody started giggling and poking each other with their elbows, because Dr. Brad said the *L* word. Anytime somebody says "love," you should start giggling and poking the person next to you with your elbow. That's the first rule of being a kid.

"*You* know vut I mean," Dr. Brad said. "If you have a disagreement viz somevon, you should try to talk it out instead of fighting about it all zuh time."

Dr. Brad got up and we all walked near the woods at the end of the playground. We're not supposed to play back there. Our principal, Mr. Klutz, once told us that he saw a big, black bear out there one day. He was probably just kidding, but I stay away from the back of the playground anyway, because I don't want to get attacked by a big, black bear.

That's when the most amazing thing in the history of the world happened!

There was a loud sound in the trees.

We all turned around.

And you'll never believe in a million hundred years what came roaring out of the woods.

No, it wasn't a big, black bear.

Ha! You thought it was a big, black bear, didn't you? Well, nah-nah-nah boo-boo on you, because it wasn't. It was a big, black *motorcycle*. A big, black, *loud* motor-cycle. And it was coming straight at us!

"*Eeek!*" shouted all the girls.

"Run for your life!" shouted Neil the nude kid.

The big, black motorcycle skidded to a stop right next to Dr. Brad. After the dust cleared, the guy riding the motorcycle took off his helmet. He had deep-blue eyes and long, dark hair. He said only one word.

"Yo."

Mr. Jack Is Cool

Is "yo" even a word?

I know that "yo-yo" is a word. I saw this guy at a toy store once who did yo-yo tricks. He could fling the thing above his head, between his legs, and all over the place. Yo-yos are cool.

Where was I? Oh, yeah, it doesn't matter if "yo" is a word or not, because the motorcycle guy said it. And if you say it, I guess, it must be a word.

"Who's *he*?" everybody was asking.

"He's *cool*," said Neil the nude kid.

"He looks like a movie star!" said Alexia.

"He's handsome!" said Andrea.

"He's *dreamy*!" said Emily.

The motorcycle guy turned off his motorcycle. He was wearing leather pants, leather shoes, a leather belt, and a leather jacket. That guy must *really* like leather! I wondered how many cows had to die to make his clothes.

He reached into his pocket and pulled out a comb. Then he started combing his hair in slow motion. Doing anything in

slow motion is cool. I saw this TV show
once where they dropped watermelons out
of a ten-story building
and you could
see them hit
the ground
and explode
in slow
motion. That
was cool.

"Excuse me, sir,"
said Dr. Brad. "May
I ask who you are
and vut you are
doing on school
property?"

The motorcycle guy didn't say anything for a long time. He just stared at Dr. Brad with his deep-blue eyes.

"My name is Mr. Jack," he finally said. "You can call me . . . Mr. Jack."

"But your *name* is Mr. Jack," said Ryan.

"I know," said Mr. Jack. "That's why you should call me Mr. Jack."

"Don't you want us to call you something *instead of* Mr. Jack?" asked Michael.

"No. Why?" asked Mr. Jack.

"When people say 'You can call me,' that usually means we should call them something *different* from their regular name," I told him.

"Not this time," said Mr. Jack.

That guy is weird.

The recess bell rang, and kids came pouring out of the school.* They must have seen the motorcycle, because a whole bunch of them came running over and gathered around Mr. Jack. So did some of the teachers.

"Well, *hello*," said our gym teacher, Miss Small. She was all giggly and she started fussing with her hair.

"Hi there, stranger," said Miss Holly, our Spanish teacher. She was blushing and started fanning herself with her hand.

"New in town?" asked Ms. Hannah, our

---

*Well, not really. You pour stuff out of a pitcher, not out of a school.

art teacher. She pulled a little mirror out of her pocket and started putting makeup on her face.

All the lady teachers were giggling and blushing and fussing with their hair and fanning themselves and looking in little mirrors. Ladies always do that stuff when they're in love. Nobody knows why. Miss Small looked like she was going to faint.

"What's your name, sugar?" asked Miss Laney, our speech teacher.

"Hello, ladies. My name is Mr. Jack. You can call me . . . Mr. Jack."

"Well," giggled Miss Holly, "you can call me . . . available."

Dr. Brad pushed his way to the front so he could talk to Mr. Jack.

"I'm sorry, sir, but vut you are doing is called trespassing," said Dr. Brad. "Zis is school property. You need to leave."

"Oh, yeah?" said Mr. Jack. "Who's gonna *make* me?"

"Ooooooooh!" we all said.

Anytime somebody says "Who's gonna make me?" you have to say *"Ooooooooh!"* That's the first rule of being a kid.

"I suppose *I'm* going to make you," said Dr. Brad.

"Oh, yeah?" said Mr. Jack. "You and what army?"

"Ooooooooh!"

Anytime somebody says "You and what army?" you have to say *"Ooooooooh!"* That's the second rule of being a kid.

"I'm scared," said Emily, who's scared of everything.

Dr. Brad was looking at Mr. Jack. Mr. Jack was looking at Dr. Brad. We were all looking at Dr. Brad and Mr. Jack. Well, the girls were pretty much just looking at Mr. Jack.

At that moment, the back door of the school opened, and a bunch of male teachers came out—Mr. Macky, Mr. Granite, Mr. Loring, Mr. Docker. Even Mr. Louie, our school crossing guard, and Mr. Tony, the after-school program director, came out. They all ran over and made a circle around Mr. Jack.

"*Zees* army!" said Dr. Brad.

"*Ooooooooooh!*"

Weapons of Mass Destruction

3

"Who *is* this guy?" asked Mr. Macky, our reading specialist.

"His name is Mr. Jack," I said. "But you can call him Mr. Jack."

"Okay, Mr. Jack," said our science teacher, Mr. Docker. "This is school property. You can't stay here. We have you outnumbered. If you won't leave on your own, we're going to have to *make* you leave."

"Oh, let him stay," said Miss Holly. "He's *cute*."

"Yeah," said all the lady teachers. "He's cute!" Then they all started giggling.

"This is going to be *cool*," Ryan whispered to me.

"Now zees is exactly zuh kind of situation I vus telling you children about," said Dr. Brad. "Vee are having a little disagreement here. Ven mature adults have disagreements, zuh best vay to settle zem is to have an open and honest discussion instead of fight—"

But Dr. Brad didn't get the chance to finish his sentence. At that moment, Mr. Jack picked him up and held him in the air.

"Eeee-yah!" screamed Mr. Jack. Then he threw Dr. Brad across the playground!

"WOW!" we all said, which is MOM upside down.

Dr. Brad landed in the bushes. It was cool! I had no idea you could throw another person so far.

Mr. Jack jumped into a karate pose.

"I must warn the rest of you fellows," he said, "these hands are dangerous tools. In fact, I had to have them registered with the government as weapons of mass destruction."

Mr. Jack's hands looked just like regular hands to me. But what do I know about karate?

"We're not afraid," said Mr. Tony. "Come on, boys. Let's *take* him!"

With that, Mr. Tony charged at Mr. Jack.

"Eeee-yah!" screamed Mr. Jack.

He spun around fast, grabbed Mr. Tony's arms, gave him a kick in the butt, and sent him tumbling to the ground.

"I don't approve of violence on school property," said Andrea.

"What do you have against violins?" I asked her.

"Not violins, Arlo!" Andrea shouted at me. "Violence!"

"Oh, that's different," I said.

Mr. Tony got up, and the other male teachers came after Mr. Jack, one at a time.

Mr. Granite jumped on Mr. Jack. Mr. Jack flipped him sideways. Mr. Granite was flat on his back.

Mr. Louie tried to grab Mr. Jack's legs. Mr. Jack jumped up and landed on Mr. Louie.

"*Eeee-yah!*" screamed Mr. Jack.

"Hide your eyes, Emily!" Andrea said. "This kind of behavior is definitely not appropriate for children."

Mr. Macky and Mr. Loring charged at Mr. Jack, but Mr. Jack grabbed both of them at the same time and bonked their heads together.

"*Eeee-yah!*" screamed Mr. Jack.

"*Oooof!*" grunted Mr. Loring as he hit the ground with a thud.

One by one, Mr. Jack kicked all their butts. It was like watching professional wrestling on TV, but without the TV.

All the lady teachers were giggling and blushing and fussing with their hair and fanning themselves and looking at their faces in little mirrors. All the male teachers were sprawled on the ground, moaning and groaning. It was hilarious.

"I guess you fellows will think twice before messing with Mr. Jack again," said Mr. Jack. Then he started combing his hair.

"How do I look?" he asked. "Does anybody want my autograph?"

Step Outside

4

You'll never believe in a million hundred years who came running out of the school at that moment. It was Mr. Klutz, our principal! He's like the president of the world.

Mr. Klutz has no hair at all. I mean *none*. They should put a solar panel on his head to generate electricity.

"What's going on out here?" Mr. Klutz demanded.

Nobody said a word. Everybody stepped out of the way.

Mr. Jack and Mr. Klutz were standing there, staring at each other. You could hear a pin drop.*

"This playground ain't big enough fer the both of us, pardner," said Mr. Jack.

"I reckon it ain't, pardner," said Mr. Klutz.

Why were they talking like it was the Wild West? That was weird.

"I don't like the sound of this," Andrea said.

---

*That is, if anyone had a pin and dropped it.

28

"Me neither," said Emily.

"I'm going to have to ask you to step outside, sir," Mr. Klutz said.

"We're already outside," Mr. Jack replied.

"Oh, yeah."

Mr. Jack turned to face us.

"Should I beat this guy up too?" he asked.

"Yeah!" shouted all the boys.

"No!" shouted all the girls.

Mr. Jack took two quick steps forward and dove at Mr. Klutz's legs, knocking him down. Then he picked up Mr. Klutz and raised him high over his head.

"Help!" Mr. Klutz shouted. "Put me down!"

"Eeee-yah!" screamed Mr. Jack.

Mr. Jack spun around a few times. Then he dropped Mr. Klutz on the ground and sat on him so he couldn't get up.

You should have been there! It was amazing!

What happened next was even *more* amazing. Mr. Jack got up and helped Mr. Klutz to his feet. They shook hands and hugged each other. Then all the male teachers came over to shake hands with Mr. Jack. So did all the lady teachers. Then *all* the teachers got in a line and took a bow, like they were in a play or something.

A few kids started clapping their hands, and then the rest of us broke into applause.

"Zank you, Zank you," said Dr. Brad. "You all did a vunderful job."

"Wait a minute!" I shouted. "You mean to say that wasn't a *real* fight?"

"No, of course not!" Dr. Brad replied. "At Ella Mentry School, vee don't fight. Vee settle our differences viz verds, not viz fists."

"I felt that you kids should learn a few

basic self-defense moves in case of emergency," Mr. Klutz told us. "It's a dangerous world out there and blah blah blah blah blah blah blah. Everyone needs to blah blah blah blah blah blah blah. That's why I hired Mr. Jack to spend the rest of the day with us."

"Hooray!" we all shouted.

"Any questions?" asked Mr. Jack.

"You're really good at karate," said Michael. "Do you have a black belt?"

"Let me put it this way," said Mr. Jack. "I *do* have a belt, and it's black."

"Wow, he has a black belt!" I shouted.

I always wanted to take karate classes, but my parents said I had to wait until I

was in fourth grade.

"Who wants to be door closer for the day?" asked Mr. Klutz as we all walked back inside the school.

"Me! Me! I do!" we all shouted.

Everybody wanted to be door closer for the day. That's an important job, because you have to be sure to close the door. If the door closer for the day doesn't close the door, a wild animal might wander into the school. So being door closer is way more important than being line leader or snack passer outer.

I always wanted to be door closer for the day. But Mr. Klutz never picks me. He always picks one of the other kids.

"A.J., you are the door closer for the day," Mr. Klutz said.

"Yes! I rule!"

After I closed the door, I ran up ahead so I could talk to Mr. Jack.

"Are you going to teach us how to beat people up?" I asked him.

"Up, down, and sideways, baby!" he replied.

This was gonna be *cool*!

5

Butt-Kicking Time

Mr. Jack led everybody into the gym. I stood between Ryan and Michael. We were all excited. We'd seen a lot of karate movies, and a lot of wrestling on TV. Finally we would get to kick some butt like those guys.

"Do we get to kick butt now?" I

asked Mr. Jack.

"First, we need to warm up with stretching exercises," Mr. Jack told us. "I don't want anyone to get hurt."

That made sense, I guess.

"Everybody reach up and touch the sky," Mr. Jack told us.

We all reached up and touched the sky.* Then we touched our toes. Then we leaned backward as far as we could go. Then we got down on the floor and twisted and turned and pulled every part of our bodies for a million hundred minutes. Then we did jumping jacks.

I thought I was gonna die! This was the

_____

*Or whatever part of the sky was right over our heads.

worst thing to happen since TV Turnoff Week.

"Okay, everybody sit on the floor 'criss-cross applesauce,'" Mr. Jack told us.

Grown-ups used to tell us to sit like a pretzel. But that didn't make any sense, because pretzels don't sit. After that, they told us to sit "crisscross applesauce." Applesauce doesn't sit either. But one time I sat *in* some applesauce in the vomitorium and got it all over my pants. It was gross.

"Let us close our eyes," Mr. Jack told us.

What? How can I kick butt with my eyes closed?

"Take a deep breath," Mr. Jack said

softly. "Now exhale. Do that again. Deep breath . . . exhale."

"Excuse me," I said. "What does this have to do with kicking butt?"

"Shhhh," Mr. Jack said. "A closed mouth gathers no feet."

"Huh? What does *that* mean?"

"It means keep quiet and you won't say anything dumb, Arlo," Andrea said. "It's a wise saying."

It didn't sound very wise to me.

"Hush," said Mr. Jack. "First you must learn how to breathe."

"I already know how to breathe," I said. "If I didn't know how to breathe, I'd be dead."

"Shhhhh," Mr. Jack said. "Sit quietly. Can you hear your heart beating?"

I listened for my heartbeat. The only thing I could hear was the ceiling fan.

"Keep your eyes closed. Stare at the inside of your eyelids," Mr. Jack told us.

I tried to stare at the inside of my eyelids, but I couldn't see anything. My eyelids had nothing on them. I wondered if everybody else was seeing cool stuff on the inside of their eyelids. I opened my eyes for a second to look, but then I couldn't see my eyelids anymore.

Somebody should tell Mr. Jack that the inside of our eyelids is really boring. They should put TV sets in there. Then

you could watch TV while you're sleeping. That would be cool.

"Think happy things," Mr. Jack said. "Allow your stress and bad feelings to escape. Today is the tomorrow you worried about yesterday."

Wow, Mr. Jack was like Yoda from *Star Wars*, but taller and with muscles.

"Become one with the universe," Mr. Jack told us. "The less you have, the more there is to get."

Huh? That didn't make any sense at all.

"Feel the energy within you," said Mr. Jack. "It's easier to wear slippers than to cover the earth with carpet."

What?

"Let your tension melt away," said Mr. Jack. "If you hit your toe with a hammer first thing in the morning, nothing worse can happen to you for the rest of the day."

Wait. *What?* I was starting to think that Mr. Jack was crazy.

"Repeat after me," he said. "I ying gah."

WHAT?!

"I ying gah," we all said, even though it made no sense at all.

"Again. I ying gah."

"I ying gah . . . I ying gah . . . I ying gah . . . I ying gah . . ."

We had to say that dumb *I ying gah* thing about a million hundred times. It was the most boring thing in the history of the world.

"Okay, open your eyes," Mr. Jack said.

Finally, it was over. What a relief!

Mr. Jack said he would be working with small groups, so our class got to stay in the gym while everybody else went to their classrooms.

"Does everyone feel relaxed now?" Mr. Jack asked us.

"Yes!" said all the girls.

"No!" said all the boys.

"We don't want to learn *that* stuff," Ryan told Mr. Jack. "We want to learn how to kick butt."

"Yeah, Mr. Klutz didn't bring you here

to teach us how to breathe and stare at our eyelids," said Alexia. "I thought you were supposed to show us how to defend ourselves in case of emergency."

"That's exactly what we're going to do," Mr. Jack replied. "Okay. Boys on one side of the gym, girls on the other."

All right! Finally it was butt-kicking time!

Michael lined up across from Alexia.

Ryan lined up across from Emily.

Neil lined up across from Annette.

And I lined up across from . . . Andrea!

Yes! Finally! After all these years of being annoyed by Andrea, I would get to show her who's boss. This was going to be the greatest day of my life.

"Oooooh!" Ryan said. "A.J. lined up across from Andrea. They must be in love!"

"When are you gonna get married?" asked Michael.

Sweet Revenge

I looked across the gym at Andrea. She was giving me the evil eye. I put on my meanest mean face. Finally I would get back at her for all the times she made fun of me. All the times she said mean things to me. All the times she did something better than me. Revenge would be *sweet*.

"You're going *down*!" I shouted, pointing at Andrea.

"I don't *think* so, Arlo," Andrea replied.

Mr. Jack went to the room where all the sports equipment is stored. He came out rolling a big cart. It was full of helmets, kneepads, elbow pads, and every other kind of pads you can think of.

"Do you have any iPads?" I asked.

"Do we really have to put all this stuff on?" asked Neil the nude kid.

"Yes," Mr. Jack replied. "We don't want anyone to get hurt."

"Why not?" I asked. "Isn't the whole point of fighting to hurt somebody?"

"We're not fighting," Mr. Jack told me.

"We're learning how to defend ourselves. There's a difference. Wise is the man who knows when he runs out of invisible ink."

What?! Mr. Jack sure knew a lot of weird wise sayings.

We all put on helmets and pads. After that, Mr. Jack took out a giant roll of plastic bubble wrap and he made us wrap ourselves up in it. He sealed it with duct tape.

I looked like a giant marshmallow. It would have been embarrassing, but *everybody* looked like giant marshmallows, so it was okay.* Mr. Jack stuck a name

---

*If one person dresses up in crazy clothes, it's weird. But if everybody dresses up in crazy clothes, it's *fashion*.

tag on each of us.

"Okay, A.J.," he said. "When I count to three, I want you to attack Andrea."

"With pleasure!" I said.

"And Andrea," said Mr. Jack, "I want you to do everything you can to defend yourself."

"Oh, I will," Andrea said. "I will!"

"One . . . two . . . *three!*"

I came charging toward Andrea at full speed. My plan was to tackle her like we do in Pee Wee football. But at the last instant, Andrea stepped aside, grabbed my legs, and flipped me over. I went flying.

"Eeee-yah!" Andrea screamed.

I don't know exactly what happened next, but when it was over, I was lying on the floor. All the girls were cheering and clapping. All the boys were giggling.

Okay, Andrea was lucky that time. Anybody can get lucky once in her life.

I got to my feet and came charging at Andrea again. This time, she bent over at the last second, pulled my arm, twisted it, and elbowed me in the stomach. Once again, I was on the floor.

"Eeee-yah!" Andrea screamed.

Okay, I must have slipped that time. It happens. I struggled to my feet and came charging at Andrea again. This time, I was careful not to let her grab me with her hands.

"Eeee-yah!"

Andrea spun around on one foot. The next thing I knew, her other foot was flying at my head. I tried to duck, but her foot caught me in the helmet and sent me reeling backward. I landed on the floor next to the bleachers.

"Nicely done, Andrea!" said Mr. Jack,

clapping his hands. "Where did you learn how to do that?"

"I take karate classes after school," Andrea said.

Now she tells me.

I should have known. Andrea takes classes in *everything* after school. If they gave classes in how to clip your toenails, she would take that class so she could get better at it.

"It looks like the shoe is on the other foot, Arlo," Andrea said, sneering at me.

Huh? What did shoes have to do with anything? I looked down at my feet to make sure I hadn't put my shoes on backward. That's when Andrea came charging at me. I put my hands up at the last second to protect my face, but she took a flying leap, and the two of us landed in a heap on the floor, with Andrea sitting on top of me. She was holding her fists up in the air and all the girls were cheering.

"Oooooh!" Ryan said. "Andrea just totally kicked A.J.'s butt! They must be in love!"

"When are you gonna get married?" asked Michael.

If those guys weren't my best friends, I would hate them.

The Key to Self-Defense

After that, we had to go back to class so the other grades could get their turn with Mr. Jack. My teacher, Mr. Granite, started talking about fractions and stuff, but I couldn't pay attention. I kept thinking about what had happened in the gym.

Not only did a girl kick my butt, but

the girl was *Andrea*. And not only did she kick my butt, but she kicked my butt with the *whole class* watching. The best day of my life had turned into the worst day of my life.

Sitting in class, I felt like everybody was looking at me and whispering. I thought I was gonna die. I wanted to run away to Antarctica and live with the penguins. Penguins don't attack each other. Penguins are nice.

After about a million hundred minutes, an announcement came over the loud-speaker. Our class had to go down to the gym again for another session with Mr. Jack. I didn't want to go, but I knew that I

had to. If I said I didn't feel well or made up some other excuse, everybody would know it was just because I didn't want Andrea to kick my butt again.

We walked to the gym in single file. In the middle of the gym floor was a machine. It looked sort of like a big vacuum cleaner or something.

"What's that, Mr. Jack?" asked Neil the nude kid.

"Oh, you'll see," Mr. Jack replied. "Let's get down to business. I want the whole class to stand on the blue line."

We all went over to the blue line. I stood between Ryan and Michael. Mr. Jack went over to the machine in the middle of the gym.

"I don't have a good feeling about this," Ryan whispered to me.

"Me neither."

"Now, the best way to defend yourself in a fight is to not get into the fight in the first place," said Mr. Jack. "Right?"

"Right!" we all said. When grown-ups say "Right?" you should always answer "Right!" That's the first rule of being a kid.

"So the key to self-defense is to avoid hand-to-hand combat," said Mr. Jack. "Right?"

"Right!"

"Sometimes you have to be quick on your feet. Right?"

"Right!"

"You have to get out of the way. Right?"

"Right!"

Mr. Jack flipped a switch on the machine. It started making a whirring sound.

"So let's see how good you are at getting

out of the way," Mr. Jack said.

He pushed a button on the machine, and you'll never believe in a million hundred years what came shooting out of it.

Ping-Pong balls!

And they were coming directly at *us*!

"Watch out!" Alexia shouted.

Ping-Pong balls were flying *everywhere*. Everybody was yelling and screaming and freaking out.

"Why are you shooting Ping-Pong balls at us?" shouted Andrea.

"To see how good you are at getting out of the way!" shouted Mr. Jack. "Stay on the blue line! Try not to get hit!"

"Ow! He got me!" screamed Emily after

a Ping-Pong ball bounced off her head.

"If you get hit, you're out of the game," Mr. Jack shouted. "Go sit on the side."

Emily started crying, and she went running out of the gym. What a crybaby.

Mr. Jack moved the Ping-Pong machine back and forth so the balls sprayed across the whole class.

"Duck! Dive! Dip! Dodge!" he yelled, with a crazy look in his eyes. "Eagles may soar, but weasels don't get sucked into jet engines."

What?! Mr. Jack is a maniac!

We were all diving out of the way, but Ryan got hit on the leg. He was out. Then Michael got hit on the arm. He was out.

Alexia got hit in the back. She was out. One by one, kids were getting nailed with Ping-Pong balls and going off to sit on the side of the gym.

"Aha-ha-ha!" yelled Mr. Jack after Neil the nude kid got hit in the chest. "Another one bites the dust!"

I was diving left and right and jumping up and down like crazy. There was only one other kid left on the blue line.

Andrea.

Mr. Jack stopped for a minute to reload the Ping-Pong ball machine. I was breathing really hard.

"Beat him again, Andrea!" shouted one of the girls.

"You can do it, A.J.!" shouted one of the boys.

"Only two kids left," Mr. Jack said excitedly. "Who will be the last one standing?"

"I'd just like to say that I don't approve of this violence," Andrea said. "It's inappropriate for children."

"What do you have against violins?" I asked.

Mr. Jack pushed the button again, and Ping-Pong balls started flying at Andrea and me, faster than ever. I dove to my left. I dove to my right. I jumped up in the air. Then I heard a *pop* as a Ping-Pong ball hit Andrea on her shoulder.

"Ouch!" she yelled. "That *hurt*!"

Everybody started cheering. Mr. Jack turned off the machine.

"You are The Man, A.J.!" Ryan shouted.

Everybody in the class came over and told me how awesome I was. Andrea gave me a hug and said, "You're my hero, Arlo!" Mr. Jack gave me a certificate that said I was a First-Class Ping-Pong Ball Avoider.

It was the greatest day of my life.

Intimidation

Mr. Jack rolled the Ping-Pong ball machine over to the corner of the gym. He told us to sit on the floor.

"Okay," he said, "the next thing you kids need to learn is *intimidation*. That's a pretty big word—five syllables. Does anybody know what it means?"

"A syllable is a part of a word," I said.

"No, dumbhead!" Michael said. "He wants to know what 'intimidation' means."

"I knew that," I lied.

Andrea waved her hand in the air like she was trying to flag down a helicopter. What a brownnoser. So of course Mr. Jack called on her.

"When you intimidate somebody, you scare them," Andrea said, looking all proud of herself.

"That's right," Mr. Jack said.*

Well, sure it was right. Andrea got one of those electronic book things for her

---

*Hey, if "intimidate" and "scare" mean the same thing, why do we need two words?

birthday, so now she can look up words all the time to show everybody how smart she is. What is her problem? Why can't a truck full of electronic books fall on Andrea's head?

"There are many ways to intimidate an attacker," Mr. Jack told us. "First, you need to know how to scream. Andrea, I heard you scream earlier. Would you please demonstrate?"

"Eeee-yah!" screamed Andrea. I covered my ears.

"Very good," said Mr. Jack. *"Eeee-yah!* It's even more intimidating if lots of people scream as a team. Let's hear the rest of you."

"Eeee-yah!" we all screamed.

"That wouldn't intimidate a fly," Mr. Jack said. "Louder!"

"Eeee-yah!" we all shrieked our heads off.

"Much better," said Mr. Jack. "That's teamwork! Next, you need to make yourself look *big*."

"How can we be any bigger than we are?" asked Alexia.

"Like this," Mr. Jack said. He raised his hands in the air and spread his legs apart. He actually looked bigger!

"Eeee-yah!" screamed Mr. Jack.

"I'm intimidated," said Emily, who is intimidated by everything.

"If an attacker thinks you're tough, he'll think twice about bothering you," Mr. Jack said. "Take off your jacket and wave it around in the air. You need to be as obnoxious as possible."

"That should be easy for you, *Arlo*," said Andrea. "You can be obnoxious without even trying."

"Your *face* is obnoxious," I told Andrea.

"Oh, snap!" said Ryan.

"If you're *really* obnoxious," Mr. Jack told us, "an attacker will think you're crazy and leave you alone. Watch . . ."

Mr. Jack started screaming *"Eeee-yah!"* and stomping around and waving his jacket and whistling.

And you'll never believe who walked into the door at that moment.

Nobody! It would hurt if you walked into a door. But you'll never believe who walked in the door*way*.

It was Mr. Klutz!

He watched Mr. Jack screaming *"Eeee-yah!"* and stomping around and waving his jacket and whistling. Then Mr. Klutz shook his head, rubbed his forehead with his fingers, and left.

"See?" Mr. Jack said. "Mr. Klutz thinks I'm crazy, so he left me alone. That's what I call intimidation!"

Mr. Jack is weird.

Don't Try This at Home

9

After we learned how to be intimidating, it was time for lunch and recess. Then we went back to our regular class.

"Let's pick up where we started this morning," Mr. Granite told us. "Turn to page twenty-three in your—"

He didn't get the chance to finish his

sentence. At that moment, Mr. Jack suddenly ran into our classroom at full speed.

"Eeee-yah!" he screamed as he leaped up on Mr. Granite's desk.

Everybody freaked out.

"Mr. Jack!" said Mr. Granite. "To what do we owe the pleasure of your company?"

That's grown-up talk for "What are *you* doing here?"

"You never know when you might get attacked," said Mr. Jack. "Always be ready for the unexpected."

"But if something is unexpected," asked Andrea, "how can we be ready for it?"

For the first time in the history of the world, I agreed with Andrea.

"Yeah," I said. "If we're ready for it, it won't be unexpected."

Mr. Jack wasn't listening. He was looking at the stuff on Mr. Granite's desk. Then he picked up a glue stick and started waving it around.

"What would you do if I attacked you right *now*?" he shouted.

"With a glue stick?" asked Ryan.*

"Are you going to glue us to death?" asked Neil the nude kid.

"*Anything* can be a weapon!" shouted Mr. Jack as he leaped off Mr. Granite's desk and shoved the glue stick in Neil's

*Watch this:

www.youtube.com/watch?v=piWCBOsJr-w

77

face. "Someone could attack you with cotton balls. Someone could attack you with Q-tips! Always expect the unexpected!"

At that moment, something even *more* unexpected happened. Our school lunch lady, Ms. LaGrange, came into the classroom. She's from France. Ms. LaGrange was wheeling a cart with a big block of ice on it.

"*Bonjour!*" said Ms. LaGrange. "Did somebody ask for a big block of ice?"

"Yes, leave it right there," Mr. Jack told her.

"What's the big block of ice for?" asked Alexia.

"To defend yourself, you need to be

tough," Mr. Jack said. "And to show you how tough I am, I will now break this block of ice in half . . . with my head."

WHAT?!

Mr. Jack stood in front of the big block of ice.

"Why would you want to do *that*, Mr. Jack?" asked Alexia.

"Yeah," I said. "What did that big block of ice ever do to *you*?"

But Mr. Jack wasn't listening. He was concentrating on the big block of ice.

"Kids, don't try this at home," he told us. "I'm a professional. I just hope I don't mess up my hair."

Mr. Jack took a few deep breaths. Then

he closed his eyes.

"Don't do it!" Andrea shouted. "You'll get hurt!"

"Yes, don't do it, Mr. Jack!" shouted Emily.

"Do you all want me to do it?" asked Mr. Jack.

"No!" shouted all the girls.

"Yes!" shouted all the boys. Breaking stuff is cool. Especially when you break stuff with your head.

It was exciting. There was electricity in the air.

Well, not really. If there had been electricity in the air, we all would have been electrocuted. But we were all glued to our seats.

Well, not exactly. It would be weird to be glued to a seat. Why would anybody do a dumb thing like that? How would you get the glue off?

"Okay, I'm going to do it," Mr. Jack said. "One . . . two . . ."

But Mr. Jack didn't get the chance to break the big block of ice with his head. Because the most amazing thing in the history of the world happened.

We got called down to the gym.

Well, that's not the amazing part, because we get called down to the gym all the time. The amazing part was what happened when we were in the gym.

But I'm not going to tell you what it was.

Okay, okay, I'll tell you.

But you have to read the next chapter. So nah-nah-nah boo-boo on you.

The Emergency

We had to walk a million hundred miles with Mr. Jack. I didn't have to be the line leader or the door holder because Mr. Klutz had already named me door closer of the day.

The whole school was in the gym. Mr. Granite made us sit boy-girl-boy-girl. So I had to sit between annoying Andrea and crybaby Emily. Ugh, disgusting!

Mr. Jack went up to the front of the gym, where Mr. Klutz, Dr. Brad, and our vice principal, Mrs. Jafee, were standing. They all held up their hands and made shut-up peace signs. We all stopped talking.

"Mr. Jack told me you kids did a great job today," Mr. Klutz announced. "So each of you will receive this self-defense certificate. Remember, the skills you learned are *only* to be used in case of an emergency."

"Zat's right," said Dr. Brad. "Vee try to avoid fighting and talk zings out venever possible."

That's when the most amazing thing in the history of the world happened.

A big, black bear walked into the gym!

Everybody started laughing, because we figured the bear was just a couple of teachers wearing a bear suit.

"Very funny," said Mrs. Jafee. "Okay, which of the teachers dressed up like a bear?"

That's when the bear got up on its hind legs.

"Rooooaaaarrrr!" roared the bear.

It wasn't some teachers wearing a bear suit. It was a *real* bear! The thing must have been ten feet tall, and it had razor-sharp claws and killer jaws!

"Ahhhhhhhhhhh!" everybody screamed.

I thought I was gonna die. We *all* thought we were gonna die.

Andrea and Emily and I were all holding on to each other. There was no place to go. The bear was in front of the door.

"Somebody call nine-one-one!" a teacher shouted.

"Run for your lives!" yelled Neil the nude kid.

"No!" shouted Dr. Brad. "Everyvun remain calm! If vee leave it alone, zuh bear von't bother us! Don't make any sudden moves!"

Everybody stopped moving. Everybody stopped talking. We all stared at the bear. The bear stared back at us. You could have heard a pin drop.

Actually, I wish I'd had a pin. I could have used it against the bear.

"Hey," Mrs. Jafee said. "The bear walked right through the door. Who was door closer for the day?"

Everybody looked at me. I tried to make myself as small as possible.

"Let's not play zuh blame game," said Dr. Brad. "Let me handle zis. At Ella Mentry School, vee alvays try to talk zings out. I vill try to reason vis zuh bear."

Dr. Brad went over to the bear.

"Now, let's be reasonable, bear," he said. "Zees is our school. You live in zuh voods. So zuh logical zing vould be for you to go back to zuh voods and us to—"

But Dr. Brad didn't get the chance to finish his sentence, because the bear suddenly picked him up and threw him across the gym!

Wow, that was the second time in a day that somebody had picked up Dr. Brad and thrown him. That had to be a record.

It was amazing! You should have been there. We got to see it live and in person.

"Ooof!" said Dr. Brad when he landed on some foam pads near the bleachers. He seemed to be okay.

The bear was looking around, like he was trying to decide who to mess with next.

"What are we going to do *now*?" somebody yelled.

"Mr. Klutz, you should take care of it," said Ryan. "You're the principal."

"What am I supposed to do?" asked Mr. Klutz, who looked as scared as anybody. "Send the bear to the principal's office?"

"You could give the bear detention," I said.

"Wave a red cloth in front of the bear," suggested Alexia. "I saw that on TV once."

"They do that with *bulls*, dumbhead," said Andrea. "Not bears!"

That's when we realized we had a real

black-belt self-defense expert right there in front of us.

"Get him, Mr. Jack!" shouted Michael. "This is just the kind of emergency you were telling us about."

"Yeah, you know karate and stuff," I said. "You can break a block of ice with your head. Show him how tough

you are, Mr. Jack!"

"Yeah!" everybody yelled. "Get him, Mr. Jack!"

"Who, me?" asked Mr. Jack, taking a step backward. "I don't know how to . . . I . . . uh . . . it's a *bear*!"

Mr. Jack looked like he was going to cry.

"You told us to expect the unexpected!"

shouted Andrea. "Well, this is unexpected! *Do* something!"

"Yeah," said Mr. Jack, "but when I told you to expect the unexpected, I wasn't expecting *this*."

"Too bad the bear doesn't have a glue stick," I said. "Then Mr. Jack would know what to do."

"Why don't you break a big block of ice over the *bear's* head?" Ryan shouted.

"I'm afraid of bears!" Mr. Jack was whimpering and sobbing.

"Come on, Mr. Jack!" said Mr. Klutz. "Man up! Go get him! You're our only hope!"

"I can't," Mr. Jack said, blubbering. "The bear will mess up my hair!"

Teamwork

The bear got up on its hind legs and let out another roar. Everybody was frozen.

Well, everybody wasn't *really* frozen. If everybody had been frozen, we would have been made out of ice cubes.

"We're all going to die!" whispered Emily. I'm sure she would have run out of the gym if the bear wasn't blocking the door.

That's when Andrea whispered in my ear.

"We've got to *do* something, Arlo!"

"We? Like *what*?" I whispered back. "What are we going to do? Leave me out of this."

"Come on!"

Andrea grabbed my hand and pulled me up. We went running over to the bear.

"We've got to intimidate the bear," Andrea told me.

"How are we gonna do *that*?"

"Eeee-yah!" she screamed. Then Andrea jumped up and karate-chopped the bear right in his stomach!

Well, the bear must not have expected *that*. He turned around angrily and took a swipe at me with his razor-sharp claws. I dove out of the way. He missed me by inches!

"We've got to make ourselves look bigger!" shouted Andrea.

She raised her hands in the air and spread her legs apart. Then she started stomping around and waving her jacket and whistling.

The bear looked at Andrea for a moment. Then it took another swipe at me. I dodged out of the way.

"Hey!" I shouted. "What are you attacking *me* for? *She's* the one who's bothering you!"

"The bear must think you're both crazy!" shouted Michael.

"They *are* crazy!" said Neil the nude kid.

The bear started swiping his claws at

me over and over again, like he was swatting flies.

I dove to my left. I dove to my right. I jumped up in the air. I wasn't going to let that bear get me.

"Duck! Dive! Dip! Dodge!" everyone was shouting at me.

"Eeee-yah!" screamed Andrea. Then she gave the bear another karate chop on his leg.

The bear must have been getting tired, because he suddenly sat down on the floor.

"I think the bear is intimidated!" Alexia shouted. *"Eeee-yah!"*

Then the whole school got up, raised

their hands in the air, and spread their legs apart. Then they started stomping around and waving their jackets and whistling.

"Eeee-yah!" everybody shrieked their heads off.

The bear whimpered once, and then he got up and lumbered out the door. I ran over and closed it behind him.

For a moment, there was silence. Nobody moved or said a word. Then everybody started hooting and hollering and cheering their heads off.

"Hooray for Andrea and A.J.!" Ryan shouted. "They intimidated the bear!"

"That's teamwork!" said Andrea.

Suddenly, Andrea did something that

was even *more* intimidating than scaring away the bear.

She gave me a kiss!

Ugh, disgusting!

12

The First Rule of Being a Kid

Right after the bear ran out of the gym, the three-o'clock bell rang. Yippee! Time to go home! We all rushed back to our classrooms to get our backpacks.

Usually I take the bus home, but I had a dentist appointment, so my mom came to pick me up.

"What did you learn in school today, A.J.?" she asked when I got in the car.

"Nothing," I said.

Whenever your mom asks you what you learned at school today, always say "Nothing." That's the first rule of being a kid.

"Oh, come on, A.J.," my mom said. "You must have learned *something* at school today."

"We learned how to fight bears," I told her.

"Very funny. What did you learn in math class?"

"We didn't have math class."

"What did you learn in science class?"

"We didn't have science class."

"What did you learn in social studies class?"

"We didn't have social studies class."

"Well, if you didn't have math, science, or social studies class," my mom asked, "what class *did* you have?"

"Bear-fighting class," I told her.

My mom rubbed her forehead with her fingers. After that, she stopped asking me what I learned in school.

Well, that's pretty much what happened. Maybe Mr. Jack will man up and stop combing his hair in slow motion. Maybe I'll get to throw a watermelon off a ten-story building. Maybe somebody else will pick up Dr. Brad and throw him somewhere. Maybe Mr. Jack will break a block of ice in half with his head. Maybe Dr. Brad will stop trying to reason with bears. Maybe Andrea will take a class to learn how to clip her toenails better.

Maybe Mr. Jack will stop shooting Ping-Pong balls at kids and attacking them with glue sticks. Maybe Mr. Klutz will put the bear in detention. Maybe they'll invent a cream so grown-ups won't have itchy foreheads anymore. Maybe Mr. Jack will stop killing cows and wearing them. Maybe they'll figure out how to put TVs inside our eyelids.

But it won't be easy!